S0-BBJ-328

DISCARDED

The
HAUNTING
of Julia

by Mary Hooper

illustrated by Maureen Gray
cover illustrated by Josh Lynch

Librarian Reviewer
Katharine Kan
Graphic novel reviewer and Library Consultant, Panama City, FL
MLS in Library and Information Studies, University of Hawaii at Manoa, HI

Reading Consultant
Elizabeth Stedem
Educator/Consultant, Colorado Springs, CO
MA in Elementary Education, University of Denver, CO

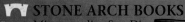 **STONE ARCH BOOKS**
Minneapolis   San Dieg

First published in the United States in 2008
by Stone Arch Books
151 Good Counsel Drive, P.O. Box 669
Mankato, Minnesota 56002
www.stonearchbooks.com

Originally published in Great Britain in 1998
by A & C Black Publishers Ltd
38 Soho Square, London, W1D 3HB

Text copyright © 1998 Mary Hooper
Illustrations copyright © 1998 Maureen Gray

All rights reserved. No part of this publication may be reproduced
in whole or in part, or stored in a retrieval system, or transmitted in any
form or by any means, electronic, mechanical, photocopying, recording,
or otherwise, without written permission of the publisher.

Library of Congress Cataloging-in-Publication Data
Hooper, Mary, 1948–
      [Thirteen Candles]
      The Haunting of Julia / by M. Hooper; illustrated by Maureen Gray.
      p. cm. — (Graphic Quest)
      Originally published as: Thirteen Candles. 1998.
      ISBN-13: 978-1-59889-827-9 (library binding)
      ISBN-10: 1-59889-827-2 (library binding)
      ISBN-13: 978-1-59889-883-5 (paperback)
      ISBN-10: 1-59889-883-3 (paperback)
      1. Graphic novels. I. Gray, Maureen, 1940– II. Title.
PN6737.H66T55 2008
741.5'973—dc22   2007006347

Summary: Before Julia can blow out her birthday candles, the flames vanish! When
she watches a replay on her dad's videotape, she sees a mysterious figure standing
behind her. Julia suspects a ghost has blown out the candles and has now come to
haunt her.

Art Director: Heather Kindseth
Graphic Designer: Brann Garvey

1 2 3 4 5 6 12 11 10 09 08 07

Printed in the United States of America

TABLE OF CONTENTS

CHAPTER ONE 5

CHAPTER TWO 28

CHAPTER THREE 44

CHAPTER FOUR 59

CHAPTER FIVE 76

CHAPTER ONE

My thirteenth birthday, July 23, was a wonderful day. There were balloons and "Happy Birthday, Julia!" banners all over the walls in the dining room. I spent the day with my mom, dad, and best friend Emma.

A CD player! Great! Thanks, Mom and Dad!

Mom had some crazy idea about having a fancy dinner for my birthday party. Otherwise, everything was perfect.

Now, isn't this lovely! Just like when you were three.

Enough already, Mom!

Well, I miss all that. I liked it when you were into balloons instead of boys.

As I said, it was a perfect day. So why was there a funny knot in my stomach? Why was there a strange tingle going up my spine?

I tried my best to ignore the feeling, but it wouldn't go away. Then in the afternoon, something really strange happened.

Okay, Julia, brace yourself. Here comes the cake!

6

When I grinned at Emma, she knew there was only one real wish for me. I wanted Simon Elkins to ask me out.

Mom put the cake on the table. She'd already embarrassed me once. Now I had to sit squirming while they sang "Happy Birthday."

Are you ready, Bill?

Ready to roll!

The camera was a recent purchase, bought especially to film my birthday and our upcoming summer vacation.

Sorry about this.

Dad turned out the lights, and Mom carefully lit the 13 birthday candles.

All set, Julia! Look at the camera and get ready to blow out the candles.

The heat from the candles was making my cheeks warm. Okay, I thought, birthday cakes are for kids. But if I'm having the cake, I might as well have the wish too. Thinking of a wish in my mind, I took a deep breath.

As Mom, Dad, and Emma started to sing, I stared at the candles—stunned.

Happy Birthday to you . . .

Maybe they were trick candles, a special kind that went out all together at the same time.

Happy Birthday to you . . .

But I knew they weren't trick candles. Mom had used some out of the same box I bought for Dad's birthday cake. Then how did they go out by themselves?

How could it happen? Maybe a sudden gust of wind blew the candles out? No. There wasn't any breeze in the room.

What, then? Had Emma blown them out for me as a joke? Not that either. The candles streamed their little blue-orange flames away from me before they went out.

The tingle ran right down my spine again, and I shivered.

Mom reached for the cake to begin cutting it.

What's up, honey? You look like you've seen a ghost.

Later, Dad filmed me and Emma getting ready to go out.

Here's my terrific daughter and her friend getting ready to hit the town.

Oh Dad, turn that thing off!

Finally, Emma and I managed to escape. We went to the local hangout, just in case there was anyone there worth talking with.

There wasn't. It seemed that anyone interesting (by that I mean Simon Elkins or Richard James) had gone away for the weekend. So, it looked like I wasn't going to get my birthday wish—at least not today.

Just our luck. What should we do now?

Let's see what's going on in the gym. Maybe there will be someone just as fun to talk to as Simon or Richard!

When we got back, Dad and Mom were waiting to watch the video of my birthday.

Take your seats, girls! Popcorn will be served during the commercial.

Dads!

Emma's dad was almost as bad as mine. She and I both knew there was no way to get out of this one. So, we settled into a cushion on the floor and waited for Dad to start the tape.

The film started in the morning with "Here's the birthday girl emerging from the covers!" . . .

. . . and continued to show the "highlights" of the day.

Oh, fantastic! Thanks, Emma! I've been wanting to read this book for ages.

19

It was all pretty boring stuff until we got to the part with the birthday cake and candles. Then the video stopped being boring and got puzzling—and scary as well.

I watched myself looking at the camera and saw myself breathe in. But then, I saw a shadow behind me—a dark, hazy shape leaning over my shoulder.

21

The film finally finished with a handwritten card.

I couldn't wait to escape though. As soon as I could, I dragged Emma up to my room.

Did you see it?

Did you see that dark thing behind me?

Emma nodded.

What do you think it was?

I don't know. Maybe just a spot on the film or something.

25

I shook my head.

No! It was something else. Something real. It blew the candles out!

Emma looked at me in disbelief.

What do you mean?

Just what I said. I didn't blow those candles out. It did.

You're crazy. What are you trying to say? Do you think it was a ghost or something?

I nodded, and I was suddenly really scared. I shivered as a tingle went down my spine.

That's exactly what I mean. A ghost.

27

CHAPTER TWO

I didn't sleep well that night. That's unusual for me. I normally drift off as soon as I close my eyes and don't budge until morning.

Instead I kept having this strange dream—or nightmare. I was being followed by a shadow that disappeared every time I turned to face it.

Several times I woke up and looked fearfully into the corners of my room, searching for shadows.

When morning finally came, Mom brought in a glass of juice. My sheets and covers, usually so smooth, were all twisted around.

Are you all right? It looks like you've been having a fight with someone.

I got dressed and went downstairs to have breakfast. While I chomped on my cornflakes, I glanced at Mom's magazine. It was open to the astrology page.

Hmm. Let's see what the stars have in store for me.

I couldn't take another bite.

I felt weird all day yesterday, then those spooky things happened, and then there had been the nightmares. Together, all of these events meant something bad would happen.

I turned the magazine around to read the whole piece.

LEO July 22–August 22

If your birthday is July 23, you're in danger of getting everything you want.

I breathed again and took another mouthful of cereal.

Julia, you're getting crazy in your old age, I thought to myself.

You're looking for trouble where there is none. The candles and the shadow were probably just a slight breeze and a trick of the light.

Emma came over later, and we decided to go shopping in town. Pretty soon we were laughing about yesterday.

33

Emma grinned and nudged me.

What's it worth not to tell Simon what sort of party you had?

You wouldn't!

I'd almost forgot the strange things that had happened yesterday, except the words "You're in danger." They kept repeating over and over inside my head. I didn't say anything to Emma. I knew she'd just think I was being silly.

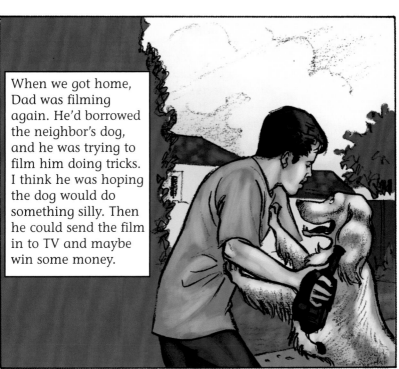

When we got home, Dad was filming again. He'd borrowed the neighbor's dog, and he was trying to film him doing tricks. I think he was hoping the dog would do something silly. Then he could send the film in to TV and maybe win some money.

When Emma and I turned up, he made us act out a crazy scene for him.

It's just for fun. I want you to take Rover here for a walk, and I'll film you going up the street.

Then what?

35

Once Mr. Film Producer of the Year had finished, we went to Emma's house for something to eat. When we got back, Dad wanted us to sit and watch the movie he'd made.

Take a seat! Take a seat! I think you're going to like this one.

With no other choice, we went into the living room and sat down in front of the TV.

When the part with Emma and I started playing, I couldn't believe what I saw.

It's there again, behind me! Look! The shadow!

Your dad is still new at taking movies. The picture will be a little out of focus while he's learning.

Do you mind? I'm a professional!

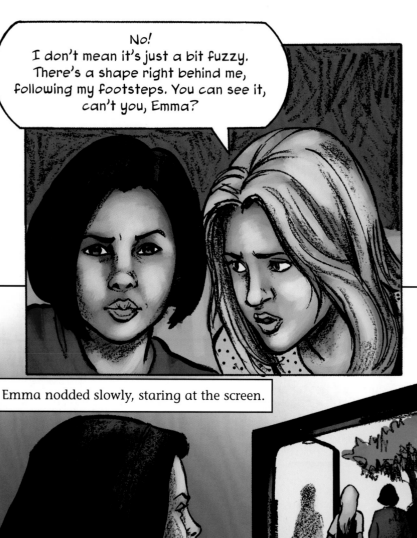

41

Emma leaned closer to the screen to get a closer look.

No, it's not. It's like you have someone standing behind you. Your double.

Just then, the film came to an end, and Mom dropped her cup of coffee.

We all looked at each other. Then, Mom rushed from the room, as if she was going to burst into tears.

What was that all about?

Your Mom's just upset because . . . because that's her best cup she broke.

I looked at Dad hard. Mom couldn't have been crying because of that cup. It was a really old cup and not her best one. No, something else had upset her. And it was something to do with that shadow.

CHAPTER THREE

Something was definitely wrong. Since my birthday, my life had changed. Mom seemed different, quieter. Several times, I caught her staring into space like something was on her mind.

I knew I wasn't imagining things, though. The shivery, frightened feeling that started on my birthday had stayed with me. Often at night, I'd lay awake with the words "You're in danger" pounding in my head.

Once, just as the clock struck three, I suddenly awoke. I sat up in bed, certain that there was someone in the room. I knew that Shadow was there.

Who's there?

What do you want?

I stared toward the window, where a street light shined dimly through my window. A blurry shape stood out against the light.

Who is it? Are you a ghost? What are you doing here?

Shadow seemed to take a step toward me, arms outstretched.

I choked back a cry of fright and turned on my bedside light. As I did, Shadow disappeared, leaving me wondering if I'd just dreamed it.

I couldn't go back to sleep. Instead, I left the light on and read until the sun came up.

I began to want to get away from the house. A couple of nights I stayed over at Emma's, and I found it much easier to sleep there.

I started looking forward to going away on vacation. It wasn't going to happen until the end of August, though, which seemed like years away.

So I was pleased when Dad said we were going to the ocean for a long weekend.

Can Emma come too?

Sure, why not?

I wasn't so pleased when we got there and it rained for two days. Emma and I just sat around watching the rain running down the windows.

If this raindrop gets to the bottom first, then Simon's going to ask me out.

No. If this raindrop gets there first, then Richard's going to ask me.

Only once did I bring up the subject of Shadow, but Emma didn't want to talk about it.

You remember that strange thing that happened on my birthday?

The only strange thing on your birthday was your mom's little kid decorations.

On the day we were going home, the wind stopped and the sun came out.

Of course, Dad got out the camera.

Okay, girls, the sun's shining. Let's play some volleyball on the beach.

He packed the camera into a bag and headed for the door.

I'll be getting out of practice with this if I'm not careful.

Emma and I put on our shorts and compared tans.

We made our way down the cliff steps to where Mom and Dad had set up camp on the sand.

Finally!

Hurry up, you two!

Coming, Mom.

Dad had made a volleyball net from part of a fence.

Okay, you two, here's the ball.

He climbed up on some rocks and shouted at us to begin.

Okay, I want lots of action.

Give us a chance to warm up.

I only want to be filmed from my best side.

You haven't got a best side!

53

I ran over to get it. The cliff cast large shadows on the beach. As I went into the shade, the sand was suddenly cold under my feet. Without the warmth of the sun, I shivered, half from the cold and half from that feeling again. I had a frightened, scary feeling someone was close to me, watching me all the time.

I paused for a moment. You're crazy, I told myself. Don't be such a baby!

I took a step toward the ball. Then I heard a strange rumbling coming from above.

I stood still and looked up. Suddenly, I saw Shadow.

It seemed to come toward me from out of the cliff, growing darker and thicker.

You're in danger!

I heard Emma and Dad shouting something, and then there was a crashing noise. I quickly curled up and felt myself being hit by a shower of small stones.

When I opened my eyes, Dad, Mom, and Emma were all racing toward me.

Are you all right?

Oh, Julia!

It was a moment before I realized what had happened. A chunk of the cliff had fallen exactly where I'd been standing. I could see a piece of the beach ball there to prove it. If Shadow hadn't shoved me out of the way, I'd have been killed.

CHAPTER FOUR

Sun or no sun, none of us could relax or enjoy the day now. Dad called the police and coast guard about the falling rocks, and then we drove straight home.

During the drive I thought things over. I didn't know what to think. Had I just dreamed up Shadow? If I had, it was a lucky dream—one which saved my life. Maybe Dad's video would give me an answer.

61

That's okay. I want to see what happens until then.

Dad thought about it for a moment, then shrugged. He popped the tape into the machine and switched it on.

The film began with Emma and me coming down
the cliff steps toward Mom and Dad on the beach.

It went blank for a second, then started again with us playing
ball, knocking it back and forth over the fence.

I watched myself run off to fetch it. Reaching the
shade, I hesitated for a moment.

Then there was a rumbling noise as rocks began to fall.

A split second later, we all gasped. We watched in disbelief as the shape of a person appeared out of nowhere and pushed me out of danger.

Then the tape went black because Dad had stopped filming.

67

I was completely puzzled. Okay, so I almost had a bad accident, but I was all right now. So why were they both acting so strange? Why was Mom crying? Then Dad spoke.

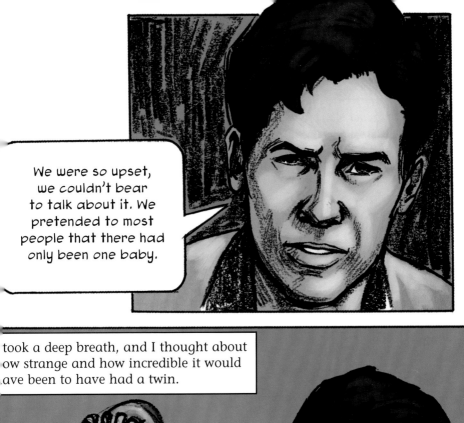

We were so upset, we couldn't bear to talk about it. We pretended to most people that there had only been one baby.

took a deep breath, and I thought about ow strange and how incredible it would ave been to have had a twin.

So now . . .

So now, well, I never would have believed it if I hadn't seen it.

73

But now maybe Joy wants to make her presence felt.

A sudden thought flashed into my head.

Of course! She didn't like being forgotten. She wants to be part of the family!

Do you think so?

Yes!

CHAPTER FIVE

When I went to bed that night, Mom came in for a chat.

I'm sorry we didn't tell you years ago. I just couldn't bear to talk about it.

That's okay, Mom. I know now.

I didn't, though. About four o'clock in the morning, I got up and went downstairs. I wanted to see the tapes again. Had Joy really grown as I'd grown? Was she really exactly like me in every way?

The films were clear, bright, and normal—no shadow, no double, no twin. I sat downstairs until the sun came up, searching the tapes for a trace of her.

She's disappeared!

But there was none.

Maybe Joy just wanted to be recognized. Maybe saving my life had been enough for her. But she was never going to be forgotten again, and the memory of her would live on. I would make sure of that.

Maybe she'll appear agai
if I'm in danger.

Only time would tell . . .

ABOUT THE AUTHOR

Mary Hooper was born in London, England. As a child, she loved visiting spooky places like castles, old houses, and graveyards. To this day, these types of frightening places inspire Hooper and help fuel her passion for writing. She has written more than 70 books, but she says, "I still have lots of ideas in my head."

GLOSSARY

astrology (uh-STROL-uh-jee)—the study of the stars and planets and how their position can affect human lives and possibly predict the future

birth certificate (BURTH sur-TIF-uh-kit)—a piece of paper that shows official information about someone's birth

coast guard (KOHST GARD)—a branch of the military that watches the sea and protects the coastline

guardian angel (GAR-dee-uhn AYN-juhl)—a spirit believed to protect a specific person

identification band (eye-den-tuh-fuh-KAY-shuhn BAND)—a bracelet or wristband worn by a newborn baby, so the hospital can immediately recognize each person

presence (PREZ-uhnss)—something felt or believed to be present, such as a spirit

puzzling (PUHZ-uhl-ing)—difficult to solve or understand

spine (SPYN)—a person's backbone

DISCUSSION QUESTIONS

1. Julia's parents kept the identical twin a secret from Julia. Do you think her parents should have told Julia the truth? Is keeping a secret ever okay? Explain your answer.

2. At the end of the story, Julia wonders if the ghost of her twin will ever return. Do you think the ghost will ever come back? Why or why not?

3. Why do you think the author chose to make Julia's ghost good instead of bad? Do you believe in ghosts? Why or why not? If so, do you think they are good or bad?

WRITING PROMPTS

1. Julia's thirteenth birthday was filled with some surprises. What was your favorite birthday? Describe the day and why it's your favorite.

2. Julia can't sleep at night because she is afraid Shadow will visit her. Write a story about something that scares you. Or, write a scary story to share with your friends.

3. When Julia first tells Emma and her parents about the ghost, they don't believe her. Write about a moment when someone didn't believe you. Why did they think you were lying?

ALSO PUBLISHED BY STONE ARCH BOOKS

Guard Dog
by Philip Wooderson

Ryan would rather play his favorite video game Guard Dog than help his dad sell his artwork at the flea market. When the artwork is stolen, however, Ryan and his friend Steve take on the case. The two boys quickly learn that a detective's work is no game.

Lost
by Chris Kreie

Every summer, Eric and his Dad head to the Boundary Waters Canoe Area in northern Minnesota. This year, Eric brought his friend Cris, and the boys want to explore the wilderness on their own. Shortly into the trip, Cris is injured, and Eric must save his friend.

Detective Files
by Steve Bowkett

Someone has stolen a priceless diamond from the city's museum! When police can't catch the crook, they call the world's most famous TV detective — Roy Kane.

Abracadabra
by Alex Gutteridge

Tom is about to come face-to-face with Charlotte, Becca's double. But there's something strange about this, because Charlotte died three hundred and fifty years ago.

STONE ARCH BOOKS,
151 Good Counsel Hill Drive, Mankato, MN 56001
1-800-421-7731
www.stonearchbooks.com

INTERNET SITES

Do you want to know more about subjects related to this book? Or are you interested in learning about other topics? Then check out FactHound, a fun, easy way to find Internet sites.

Our investigative staff has already sniffed out great sites for you!

Here's how to use FactHound:

1. Visit *www.facthound.com*

2. Select your grade level.

3. To learn more about subjects related to this book, type in the book's ISBN number: 1598898279.

4. Click the Fetch It button.

FactHound will fetch the best Internet sites for you.

Simsbury Public Library
Children's Room
Hopmeadow Street
Simsbury CT 06070